HANDMADE HOLIDAYS

'NATHAN BURGOINE

HANDMADE HOLIDAYS

Dominant Trident Publishing

CONTENTS

CONTENTS

For all my fellow Misfit Toys,
and all the trees we filled.

FIRST CHRISTMAS

Nick shouldered his way through the door of his apartment and barely managed to manoeuvre the heavy and awkwardly long box he carried through the narrow entrance. He shuffled forward—his glasses fogged over—and cursed when the box hit something, shoving it back hard into his stomach.

Nick lowered it, setting the box down between his boots, and managed to close the door behind him.

He exhaled.

After shucking off his coat and his hat, he wiped his glasses on his shirt. Finally able to see, he lugged the box around the single corner in his bachelor pad and laid it out in the so-called "living area" opposite the tiny kitchenette.

"Merry Christmas," he said.

The box contained a fake Christmas tree. It was actually a pretty nice one. It would have been expensive, but it was the floor model, as well as the last one the store had, and given that Christmas was tomorrow, they'd slashed it down to a quarter of its price. The Christmas-themed store that had opened at the other end of the mall where Nick worked would be gone by the end of Boxing Week.

Nick took a few seconds to put his coat up on the hook and then undid his boots. He filled up his kettle—a thrift store castoff—and put it on the finicky oven to boil. The Christmas Eve shift at Book It had kicked his ass. It was time for coffee. He'd been picking up as many shifts as he could—Christmas retail being the season for staff to get sick, have exams, or just plain want time off—and his boss, Tracey, knew she could rely on him. If she called, he dropped whatever he was doing and came in. Which was how he'd ended up working eleven days in a row, including this last shift, where he'd stayed two hours after the mall had closed to help set up for Boxing Day.

Which he would also be working.

But that was in two days. He had tonight to himself, and all of tomorrow, too, before he had to face going back to work. The next two pay cheques would make it all worthwhile.

The box hadn't closed properly when the clerks had tried to pack it up for him on his lunch break, and he'd told them not to worry. They'd just shoved in all the branches and the stand and then used packing tape to keep it closed. The end result was a lumpy mess, so he used a knife to cut the tape free.

If he was going to be on his own for Christmas for the first time ever—not to mention the foreseeable future—he was at least going to have a Christmas tree, dammit. He was nineteen. An adult. He could do this.

The apartment buzzer went off, startling him. He opened his door and crouched down. One of the only benefits of being in the apartment right above the entrance was being able to see through to the front door. Just outside the glass door was a figure in a puffy brown jacket, red scarf, and a black knit cap. Between the cap and the scarf, it wasn't actually possible to tell who it was, but Nick smiled, knowing only one person who'd drop by unannounced on Christmas Eve. It had to be Haruto, checking up on him.

Nick slipped on his runners and jogged down the single flight.

"Perfect timing. I just got home," Nick said.

"Ouch," Haruto said, pulling off his mitts. "I thought the mall closed at five?"

"Two hours of setting up for Boxing Day, a half-hour wait for the bus—reduced holiday schedule—and voila! I just got home."

They climbed the stairs together, and Nick held the door open for Haruto when they got to his apartment. The kettle started to whistle as Nick stepped in after him, and he went to the stove to pull it off the ring.

"Coffee?"

"You always know what to say," Haruto said. By the time he'd pulled off his coat and scarf and undone his boots, Nick had two mugs ready. He put a splash of milk in Haruto's and a teaspoon of sugar into his own. Turning, he grinned when he saw Haruto sans hat.

"You like?"

Haruto's hair was dyed with two bright streaks: one green, one red.

"Very festive."

"Thank you." Haruto bowed and then took the mug. "What's that?" He nodded at the box.

"A Christmas tree. As I am uninvited from this and all future Christmases with the Wilsons, it behoved me to get my own Christmas tree." He tried not to sound bitter. He failed.

"It looks huge."

"It's as tall as me."

"In this place?" Haruto looked around the apartment.

Nick shrugged. It was a fair question. His bachelor pad was tiny. He'd been lucky to find something he could afford, when everything had hit the fan, but he actually hadn't minded that much. Sure, the whole space—kitchen and bathroom included—was probably the same size as his bedroom at his folks', but it was close to a major bus route, so he could walk to groceries, and it wasn't like he'd had any belongings. With the hours ramping up as Christmas got closer, he'd finally managed to save up for a twin bed and mattress and had gathered castoffs to make up some of the rest. He had a pretty comfy two-seater couch and a small television. Post-Christmas, he was hoping to get himself a computer to put on the small desk he'd rescued from a curb.

"It'll class the place up a bit," Nick said.

Haruto smiled and drank some coffee. "If you say so. Oh, hey…" He put the mug on the kitchen counter and went back to the door. He rummaged in his backpack and pulled out a package wrapped in pale-blue paper, before handing it to Nick.

"Merry Christmas," he said.

Nick felt a tightness in his chest, and his throat ached. He swallowed. "You didn't have to get me a present."

"It's barely anything. I promise," Haruto said. "Seriously, open it."

Nick carefully undid the wrapping paper, sliding his finger under the tape.

Haruto sighed. "Of course you're not a shredder."

Nick didn't dignify that with a response. When he freed the box from the paper, though, he smiled. It was a box of small individually wrapped candy canes.

"Candy," Nick said. "How did you know?"

Haruto laughed. Nick's sweet tooth was notorious. "You're funny. You want help with the tree?"

"Hell yes."

They spent twenty minutes assembling the tree—the instructions weren't in the box, but letters labelled the branches and they eventually figured it out. With the tree finally assembled, Haruto helped him shove it as far into one corner of the room as possible.

It loomed there.

"It's not subtle," Haruto said before rubbing his hands together. "Right. Ornaments?"

The spark of fun and lightheartedness Nick had started to feel while they'd assembled the tree died. He closed his eyes. "I am so *stupid.*"

"What's wrong?" Haruto said.

"I don't *have* ornaments. I don't have *anything*. Because my parents..." He exhaled and opened his eyes. "I can't believe I bought a fucking Christmas tree and didn't think to get any fucking ornaments." He shook his head, fighting tears. He would *not* cry again over those people. "I'm an idiot."

"Stop." Haruto lifted his arms. "Come here."

"I don't need a hug. I need Christmas ornaments."

"You need both, Nicky, but all I've got's a hug."

Nick chuckled. He took a step forward and let Haruto give him a squeeze.

"Better?"

"Little bit," Nick said. He was quite a bit taller than Haruto, and he rested his chin on Haruto's head. He was so damn lucky Haruto was here, or that horrible moment of realization would have come alone, and he'd had more than enough horrible alone moments, frankly. Hugs would definitely do, in place of ornaments. Cute, stylish Haruto had been amazing while

Nick's life had fallen apart. The box of candy canes was just the latest in a string of small things that made his new and terrifying life of flying solo a shade less frightening.

The box of candy canes.

"Wait," Nick said, pulling back. "Yes I do."

"Pardon?"

Nick went to the counter and picked up the box of candy canes. "You brought ornaments."

Haruto smiled. "I did. I'm a genius. And I can do you one better, if you can handle me cutting the wrapping."

Nick blinked. "Come again?"

"Give me the paper," Haruto said.

Nick handed him the blue wrapping paper and headed for the tree. He started putting the candy canes on the branches. He'd have to ignore the back of the tree, and Lord knew he'd eat half of them before Boxing Day, but... It could be cool, right?

He turned and saw that Haruto had unfolded the paper and then refolded it to make a square, tearing off the excess. He started to fold it, and while Nick was hanging the candy canes, Haruto made him a paper crane.

"Ta-da," he said.

"I didn't know you did origami."

"I *so* don't. But I *can* do cranes. My mother and I folded a thousand paper cranes before she got remarried," Haruto said.

"Seriously? A thousand?"

"It's a thing." Haruto waved it off. "You got a hook or something?"

Nick thought about it for a second and then went to the cupboard under his sink. He came back with a garbage bag twist tie, and Haruto looped it around the neck of the crane, twisting it into a hook.

"Gruesome. It looks like he hung himself," Nick said when Haruto put it on the tree.

"Pretend it's a little scarf," Haruto said. "Besides, handmade gifts have heart."

They sat on the couch and had another cup of coffee, just looking at the tree. Sparsely decorated with candy canes and a single paper crane, it wasn't exactly majestic.

Nick snorted. "It's pretty pathetic, eh?"

Haruto leaned over and bumped shoulders with him. "Next year, I'm sure it'll be fabulous. Just like us." Then he sighed. "I have to head home. You okay?"

Nick looked at his sad tree again. It was a good tree, sure, but it was practically bare, the candy canes were so sparse. The paper crane, though, made him smile. It was just so Haruto to do that. Maybe his life was a little bare, too, but...

"I think so," he said.

"Merry Christmas," Haruto said.

"Merry Christmas."

After Haruto left, Nick made himself a box of mac and cheese and went back to his couch. Out the window, he caught sight of a star. It must have stopped snowing. It wasn't the first star of the evening by any means, but desperate measures and all that.

Nick Wilson made a wish.

SECOND CHRISTMAS

"I think I prefer the Muppet version," Matt said, staring at the small television, where Alastair Sim was cowering from the Ghost of Christmas Yet-to-Come.

"Don't say that too loud," Haruto said. "Or Nick will make you leave."

"I heard you and you couldn't be more wrong," Nick said, handing Matt a box of candy canes. "Here. Use these to fill up the tree."

Matt eyed the Christmas tree. "It's a bit big for your apartment, don't you think?"

"You've been feeding him lines," Nick said, narrowing his eyes at Haruto.

"Innocent until proven guilty," Haruto said. He smiled. "I like the ornaments." The tree was decorated with about two-dozen white Christmas ornaments, just simple frosted balls, but hung on the tree with loops of red ribbons. Nick had also picked up two strands of lights, and a white star that lit up for the top of the tree. They were dollar-store ornaments, but it worked.

"What's this?" Matt asked. He held out the blue paper crane.

"That's his first and most fabulous ornament," Haruto said.

Nick laughed. "Absolutely. It goes on the tree."

Matt shrugged and rehung the crane before going back to hanging the candy canes. Nick noticed he already had one unwrapped and in his mouth, too, but wasn't really surprised. Matt was a fellow sugar junkie. They'd met in line at Bittersweets before work, and both had gotten a big cookie covered in icing. Matt worked at the other end of the downtown mall from Nick, at one of the clothing stores—they'd bonded over their name tags and the ever-insane Christmas traffic, and after they'd bumped into each other a couple of times, Nick had asked him if he had enough time off to head home for Christmas.

The look on Matt's face had been like staring in a mirror.

So he'd invited him over. It had been on the spur of the moment, but once he'd done it, it occurred to him that it was actually a *great* idea. Christmas Eve for the Misfit Toys, he called it and connected with Haruto and some of the other people he'd met at the LGBT Centre in the Village. Over the last year, the Centre had become like a second home.

He was by no means the only one who wasn't heading home for Christmas. Most of the people—he and Matt notwithstanding—weren't *persona non grata* with their families but had other reasons. Haruto's mother and stepfather were spending Christmas with his eldest stepbrother this year in Vancouver, and though Haruto might have been able to swing visiting his father if he'd spent most of his time on Christmas Eve driving back to the small town where he'd grown up, as Haruto had put it, "I'd rather have rectal warts."

It wasn't his dad—it was the town. No fond memories there.

The door buzzed, and Nick left Haruto and Matt with the tree and went down the stairs. His other two guests, Fiona and Perry, had arrived. Nick adored Fiona. She was a sports therapist student he'd met at the LGBT Centre, and upon learning how his parents had cut him off completely, Fiona had raised her hand to offer him a high five. He'd been so surprised at the gesture that he'd done the same, and after they'd slapped their hands together, Fiona had said, "Welcome to the curb club." She was wearing a fuzzy Santa hat and held up two bottles.

"I brought rum, and I brought gin. If you've got Coke or tonic, I'm set. If you don't, I'll drink it straight up and blame you for the hangover."

"I have Coke," Nick said, laughing. "Come on up. Hi, Perry."

"Hi." Perry smiled. He was also from the Centre, and though Nick didn't know a ton about him, he'd made a blanket invitation for anyone with nowhere else to go. Perry, despite his impressive height, was a quiet one.

Nick led them upstairs, and once they'd shed their coats and boots, the five of them gathered around the couch. Nick sat on the floor. Haruto and Fiona sat beside each other on Nick's bed, and Perry and Matt shared the couch.

"Please tell me we're not just going to watch depressing Christmas movies," Fiona said.

"*A Christmas Carol* is not depressing," Haruto said.

"There's, like, two women in it. And one of them dies."

"It's Dickens. Of course people die."

"Not Scrooge. He gets a valuable second chance. Not that he deserves it. And his girlfriend? She gets to live out her life taking care of poor people. He doesn't go get her and say, 'Woah, hey, sorry I dumped you. Wanna come live in luxury with me?' Oh no, he just perves out on the little boy."

Perry was staring at Fiona with his mouth open.

"I can't believe you just ruined *A Christmas Carol*," Nick said.

"Wait until I explain the date rape song."

Nick blinked. "What?"

"'Baby, It's Cold Outside.' The date rape song."

"I think it's time for the rum," Nick said. "Let me get the Coke." He got up and went to the kitchen, opening his fridge and pulling out the large plastic bottle. He opened the cupboard and started putting his various mismatched glasses on the counter.

Haruto joined him, bringing Fiona's bottle of rum.

"I like her," he said. "She's fun."

"I think Perry is going to pass out," Nick said.

"He could use a little loosening up," Haruto said. "Also, here." He put a small box on the kitchen counter.

Nick regarded it. "I thought we said no gifts." Neither of them could afford much, and they'd both agreed to skip presents. Now Haruto had gone and broken the rules.

"I couldn't resist," Haruto said. "Open. Now."

Nick picked up the box and slid his finger under the paper, knowing it would annoy Haruto. He worked the box free without ripping the paper and opened the lid. Inside, on a pile of cotton balls, was a ceramic ornament. It was a mouse in a Santa hat, sitting in front of a tiny typewriter, with a piece of paper that said, 'Once Upon a Time...'

"It's you, writing your stories. And for your return to university come the new year."

"Only part-time."

"It counts."

"Sorry. You're right. It does. Hey, did you paint this?"

"Guilty. Sculpted, too—3D art project, so it pulled double duty for an assignment."

"Okay, it's adorable," Nick said. He gave Haruto a hug. "Thank you." He pulled the ornament out of the box and carried it back with the first two drinks he'd mixed. He handed one to Fiona and one to Perry and then took a second to hang the mouse on the tree. Haruto passed a drink to Matt and sat back down again.

Nick went back to the kitchen to get the last drink for himself and paused, watching his odd little group of friends.

"You think he's threatening her to make her stay?" Matt asked.

Fiona nodded emphatically. "First, he slips her a mickey. Then he suggests she could get fatal pneumonia. He's totally threatening her."

Nick grinned and headed back to join them.

"Fiona, stop ruining Christmas. Matt, don't encourage her. Perry, if you want to run away now, none of us will judge you."

"But we *will* talk about you after you go," Haruto said.

"It's true. No one dishes dirt like fags and dykes," Fiona said.

Perry surprised Nick by laughing. He had a great laugh—like everything else about him, it was a surprise. "No," he said. "I'm good. This is nice."

They settled in to watch the rest of the movie.

"I still say the Muppet version is better," Matt said.

"That's because Miss Piggy's in it," Fiona said.

FOURTH CHRISTMAS

"Let me be the first to say what we're all thinking," Fiona said. "This apartment is so much better than your other shitty place."

"Hear, hear," Haruto said, lifting his glass.

"Why do I keep inviting you?" Nick crossed his arms.

She stuck out her tongue at him, flashing her piercing. "Because I bring the hotties," she said, in a soft voice.

Nick nudged her and glanced back at the co-worker she'd brought with her. They both worked at the same gym, and Nick had to admit, the guy was indeed a hottie.

"Oh sure," Haruto said. "If you go for tall, athletic, Scandinavian types with perfect teeth."

That about summed up Erik. "I don't think he would have fit in the old apartment," Nick said.

"Honey," Haruto said. "*We* didn't fit in the old apartment. We just made it work because you and Matt are always working so late and we didn't want to make you haul your cookies to somewhere nice." When Nick smiled at him, Haruto took a sip of his drink, eyebrows high. "But yes. He's a big, lovely man."

"At least now you're making the big bucks," Fiona said.

Nick laughed. "Right. I'm the assistant manager. Those bucks are *not* big." But it was nice to finally ditch the bachelor pad for something with an actual bedroom. And his new store was closer, though he missed Tracey and the crew he'd worked with for three years. "But I like the store. The staff are good, too."

"Erik reads a lot," Fiona said. "That's why I thought you two might get along."

"You know, I think I already knew that about him," Haruto said.

Fiona frowned at him, before raising her voice. "Hey, Erik, come here. Nick will tell you the next ten books you need to read."

Nick grimaced, his back to Erik, and she winked at him.

"Come on, Ru," Fiona said. "I think it's time to start trimming the tree."

"Sure," Haruto said, though it didn't sound as upbeat as usual. Nick glanced at him.

"You okay?" he asked.

But Haruto just waved as Fiona pulled him away. And

then, suddenly, there was a big blond hunk in front of him.

"Thanks for letting me come," he said. Even his voice was butch. He was older than Nick, Nick realized, and definitely in better shape.

"Christmas for the Misfit Toys is a pretty high-class affair, but I trust Fiona when she suggests additions to the guest list," Nick said.

Erik blinked. "Misfit Toys?"

"It's from that Rudolph special. It's a thing... A few of us weren't welcome at home, so..." Nick shrugged. "It sort of evolved. Now we get together on Christmas Eve, and we decorate my tree and basically try to rescue the holiday spirit." He paused. "Except for Fiona. Fiona tries to murder the holiday spirit."

Erik laughed. "Try working with her. Every time this one song comes on, she goes nuts about patriarchy and rape culture."

"'Baby, It's Cold Outside'?"

Erik nodded. "That's the one."

Nick leaned in and lowered his voice. "It's coming up on the playlist."

Erik laughed again. "You're braver than I am."

Nick smiled. Okay, this wasn't so bad. The hot blond guy was talking to him like he wasn't slumming. That was good.

"Fiona says you write?"

Nick blushed. "Short stories. Yeah."

"Professionally?" Erik asked.

"I've sent some out, but so far…" Nick shrugged. "No bites. I got a really nice rejection letter, though. Those are good. I'm working on an English lit degree, part-time. Not in the fall, because retail Christmas, but the second term and over summer I sneak in classes as I can afford them. I figure if I keep reading, I'll get better."

Erik smiled. He had great little smile lines around his eyes. Again, Nick wondered how old Erik was. Was he over thirty? If he was, it was a *very* good thirty.

"Our rush is January," Erik said. "When remorse hits."

Nick laughed. "Guilty. I know I've joined the gym in January before."

"You didn't join mine," Erik said. "I'd have kept you."

Oh my. Was he blushing? He was pretty sure he was blushing.

"It's time, folks!" Matt called out. He and Perry had been messing with a deck of cards and had a small pile in front of them. "Come and get your card."

"Card?" Erik asked.

"It's for the ornament game. Did Fiona tell you about that?" He turned to Fiona and Haruto, who'd left the tree half covered in candy canes and white ornaments to go get their cards. "Did you warn Erik about this?"

"No," Fiona said. "I didn't want to scare him with how weird you are. But I brought two ornaments so he can play."

Erik shrugged. "I'm up for it."

"Here," Perry said, handing Erik a card. He didn't

meet Erik's eyes. Perry was too thin, Nick thought, and made a mental note to corner him. Nick had been so crazy with work the last two months, he'd barely seen anyone, and Perry was being even more quiet than normal, if that was possible.

"What'd you get?" Fiona asked Erik.

"I'm a nine," Erik said, holding up the nine of spades. If he had no idea what they were doing, he seemed okay with it.

No, I'd give you a ten, Nick thought, biting his bottom lip.

"Highest first," Matt said.

"I'm the queen," Haruto said, holding up the queen of spades.

"Of course you are," Fiona said. Haruto ignored her, and when it was obvious no one had a king, he grabbed one of the small wrapped boxes on the table.

"When your number comes up, you get to pick an ornament off the pile," Nick explained to Erik, while Haruto shredded the wrapping paper. "Or, if you like something someone else already has, you can take it from them, and they get to do the same thing—open a new present, or take something someone else has. But the ornaments can't change hands more than once a round. Once they're all open, you trade instead, or you can keep the one you've got. You're in the deck three times."

Erik nodded. "Okay."

"It can get pretty cutthroat if there's one ornament everyone wants, but it's all in good fun," Nick said.

"Says the guy who stole my rainbow unicorn kitten," Matt said.

"It was fate," Nick said. "You'll notice she's front and centre on the tree."

"She'd be happier with me," Matt said.

Haruto opened his box and revealed a drunken Santa holding out his hand and giving them all the finger.

"Well, now we know which ornament Fiona brought," Haruto said.

"It could have been any of you," Fiona said.

"Right."

Nick thought Haruto didn't sound like his usual bubbly self, either. His mother was in Vancouver again—it was his stepbrother's turn with his mother and stepfather. Maybe that was it.

Haruto drew a card, and it was a seven, which was Nick. He pulled out a package—he wanted nothing to do with surly Santa—and carefully removed the paper (mostly to tease Fiona and Haruto) before revealing a cute little caterpillar with a ball of red yarn, knitting itself a cocoon.

Nick smiled. "This is cute."

"I brought that one," Matt said. He put his arm around Perry, and Perry looked at him. Nick wasn't entirely sure, but he thought Perry might be on the edge of tears. Something was definitely going on there.

Nine was next. Erik stole the surly Santa, which let

Haruto dive back into the pile. By the time all the boxes were opened and the last card was drawn—which was Matt—everyone was in a good mood and the surly Santa had been the most-traded item, mostly between Erik and Matt. But Matt surprised Nick by taking the ornament Perry had—a red-and-green disco ball—and Perry traded the caterpillar with Fiona by giving her a purple high-heeled shoe ornament.

"A fuchsia fuck-me boot? I'll keep it," Fiona said, ending the game. "All right, let's finish caning the tree, and then we can watch *Scrooged.*"

Everyone moved to help, and Erik gave Nick a big smile before joining the others at the tree. Nick liked his little smiling marshmallow-on-a-stick ornament. He rose, but noticed Perry, who was still on the couch, was looking down at the little caterpillar, completely still.

"Perry?" he said, sitting beside him.

"Hi," Perry said, smiling. The smile, though, didn't seem genuine. He looked exhausted. Nick wondered if he'd been talking with his mother again. That woman seemed to drain the life right out of Perry, even on her best days, and she didn't have many of them.

"So, I'm just going to say it," Nick said. "I'm worried about you. Are you okay?"

"This was for me," Perry said. He held up the caterpillar. "That's why Matt brought it. We talked."

Nick didn't follow. "Pardon?"

"I told him last week," Perry sighed and looked up. He took a deep breath. "I was going to make kind of an announcement, but Fiona brought Erik, and I don't know him, so…"

"Are you okay?" Nick felt a stab of worry. Was Perry sick?

"Oh, I'm fine," Perry said. "I'm dropping out of the accounting program, and I got in at the fashion design school. Oh, and I'm not gay." He said this last with a small smile, like he'd been dying to say it.

Wait. What? Nick blinked. "Pardon?"

"I'm straight. I was sure I was gay, because…" He sighed. "You know I've been working with a therapist, right?"

Nick just nodded, waiting.

"Well, here's the thing," Perry said. "I'm a woman." He looked over at the others, who were laughing and opening their third box of candy canes. The tree was practically drowning in spun sugar. "I'm done not being me, and I'm so tired of fighting it and hiding it. I know my mother is going to have a complete shit fit, but too damn bad."

There was iron in Perry's voice. He'd never heard Perry like this before. Sure, Perry seemed tired, but…

Nick didn't have the slightest idea what to say. Nothing he could think of felt like enough. So he offered a hug.

Perry let him. "I'm worried," Perry said "My dad could barely handle me as a gay man. Can you imagine what he'll do?" Perry didn't finish the thought. "I have a plan, though. Matt's going to let me move in, if it comes to it.

Watching you guys helps, you know? You, Fiona, and Matt are fine on your own. And the trans group at the Centre? They've been amazing."

"We're not on our own," Nick said. "And neither are you."

Perry held up the small caterpillar and smiled at Nick. "If they don't want a daughter, they can fuck right off."

Nick squeezed tight.

"You're one of the bravest women I've ever met."

FIFTH CHRISTMAS

"Did Fiona say what time they'd be here?" Nick asked.

"I'm sure they'll be here soon," Erik said. "Relax."

Nick exhaled. "Sorry. I guess I want this to be perfect. It's kind of a housewarming, too, in a way."

Erik rose and crossed the living room. He wrapped his arms around Nick and pulled him in for a tight hug. "You're adorkable."

Nick kissed him. When Erik's hands wandered lower and squeezed his butt, Nick pushed back, raising an eyebrow. "We have guests coming any second."

"We could always cancel. Say that something came up," Erik said, rubbing against him and letting him feel exactly what had come up. And oh, that was a little bit tempting.

"It's too late," Nick said. "But I promise I'll make it worth your while after everyone's gone. The Misfit Toys are important. I don't have many traditions. It matters."

"I know it's important to you. That's why our tree is still empty and has no theme," Erik said.

"Theme trees are overrated."

"You're wrong." Erik gave his ass another squeeze. "But I'll show you the error of your ways later."

Nick opened his mouth in rebuttal, but the doorbell rang. "They're here."

He watched in amusement as Erik adjusted himself before heading to the door. Nick glanced around the living room, taking a deep breath. It still felt alien, even after the last three weeks, to be living in Erik's house, but he was sure he'd start to feel like this was his place soon. This party would help. Erik's friends were pretty nice to him, though he sometimes felt like they considered him a bit of a child. The decade between him and Erik didn't seem like much when he was alone with Erik, but when Erik's friends were involved...

He shook his head, banishing the thought as Fiona; her new girlfriend, Jenn; Matt; Matt's boyfriend, Johnny; Haruto; and Phoebe all piled in together. Phoebe had a high femme thing going on, with a flowing cream dress—probably one of her own designs—and bright-red shawl and lipstick to match. Her hair was longer than the last time Nick had seen her—which he realized was far too long ago. She looked wonderful. He needed to catch up with her something fierce.

"I feel like we're in hostile territory," Fiona said, holding up a bottle of white wine. "I brought libation. Maybe we can forget we're unwelcome queers in Babyhaven."

"It's Barrhaven, not Stepford," Matt said.

"Did you see all the minivans?" Fiona said. "Robot wives drive minivans. Minivans loaded with drooling, drippy babies." She looked at Erik and handed him the bottle. "Open this and pour it before my uterus revolts and decides to join the cult."

Erik saluted. "Yes, ma'am."

Was it just Nick, or did they seem a bit cool to each other? Fiona had left Erik's gym and was working in a different place now, the one in the Village, but Erik had said they were on good terms. Seeing Fiona's stiff smile, now he wasn't so sure.

Nick turned to Phoebe and opened his arms. "Love the hair, lady." Phoebe gave him a big hug.

"Thank you," she said. It struck him as wonderful all over again to hear her voice: confident, sure, and so very Phoebe. This Christmas was in many ways Phoebe's first, and he wanted her to have a great time.

"And how are my boys?" Nick asked, stepping back to trade hugs with Matt and Johnny.

"Tired," Matt said, "But ready to get cutthroat." He held up a plastic bag, and Nick grinned to see all the small, wrapped boxes inside. "I've explained the strat-egy to Johnny," Matt said. "So this year's rainbow uni-corn kitty will be mine."

"So competitive," Haruto said, nudging them aside. "C'mere."

They hugged while the rest of the group worked their way farther into the house.

"Hi, you," Nick said.

"Hi, yourself, jerk. When was the last time we hung out?" Haruto said.

Nick cringed. "I know, I know. It's just…"

"It's just you moved into the castle with your Scandinavian prince, so you're done with the little people." He waved a theatrical hand. "We know."

Nick rolled his eyes. "Yes, that's totally it. Fetch my slippers, peasant."

"Bitch," Haruto said.

"I learned from the best," Nick said.

They smiled.

"For serious, though? Too long. I miss you. Just because you've got wild monkey sex on tap doesn't mean you get to vanish, mister."

Nick nodded. "I know. I'm sorry. I'll do better."

"Hm," Haruto said, but he seemed to let it go. "So, I like Jenn. She doesn't put up with much of Fiona's shit. All the way here, she was telling her to slow the hell down."

Nick laughed. "Awesome."

They made their way back to the group, who were looking around the living room.

"You've got great light in here," Phoebe said. "And I love the colour." She smiled at Erik.

"Thanks," Erik said. His smile was strained. Nick tried not to flinch. Erik had a way to go with feeling comfortable around Phoebe, and Phoebe called Erik out hard on any transphobic bullshit, but at least so far, they were both trying. Another Christmas miracle.

"Your tree looks good here," Fiona said. "Did anything else of yours make it out onto display?"

"Most of my stuff was pretty much junk compared to his," Nick said, coming up beside Erik and putting an arm around his waist. "Though it was my bottle opener that just got you your wine."

"Well, that's something," she said.

Jenn nudged her, and Fiona took a drink of her wine.

This wasn't exactly the most fun they'd all had. There was an edge to Fiona's words.

Matt came to the rescue. "Shall we start the game?" He held up a deck of cards.

"Absolutely," Nick said. They gathered around the table, and the game began. By the time it was over, they'd all relaxed somewhat, and the laughter that was filling the room wasn't as forced or out of place. Nick went back into the kitchen. Fiona's bottle of white had run out, and he wanted to open another.

Haruto followed him a few moments later.

"I have something for you," Haruto said. "And I figured I'd pass it to you on the down-low."

Nick raised an eyebrow. "Is it salacious? I'm hoping it's salacious."

"Not really," Haruto said, and he handed Nick a wrapped box. It was small, and obviously an ornament.

"I didn't want this in the trading game because you know Fiona would have done anything she could to keep it from you."

"Aw," Nick said and flipped the small box to find the edge of the tape.

"Anyway," Haruto said. "I need to go. I wanted to make sure I dropped that off and got to see you for the brief moment I seem to be allowed, but my mother will lay an egg if I'm not there in time for dinner."

Nick sighed and put the small box on the table. "I'm sorry I haven't been around much. Between work and moving in, and all of this..." He raised his hand, as if the whole house was something on his to-do list.

"Are you okay?" Haruto asked.

"I feel like a house guest. I wasn't lying when I told Fiona that everything Erik has was better than my stuff, but it makes this place feel like his, not ours. I mean, the man owns a gym. He's had this place for three years already. It's very...*him*."

"It'll feel like yours when you add some touches. Like, say, getting rid of that awful red paint in the living room. Phoebe was being polite. That shit's *hideous*."

Nick grinned. "Right?"

"I do need to go," Haruto said. "And you need to make time for me. For all of us."

"I will."

They hugged, and Haruto left. Nick picked up the small package and finished opening it, pulling out a small ceramic ornament. His breath caught when he flipped it over. Haruto must have had the ornament made specially for him. It was the cover from the book of short stories that Nick had appeared in last spring—his first-ever published short story.

He carried it, and the wine, back into the living room.

"Well, maybe after your party you could join us all on the hill?" Fiona was saying.

"Maybe," Erik said.

"What's that?" Nick asked.

"We wanted to ask you guys to come with us to the New Year's party on Parliament Hill," Jenn said. She smiled. "I work with the NCC, and it's going to be a good show this year."

Nick refilled glasses. "That sounds like fun."

"We've got that New Year's party with the Stephen Bees," Erik said.

"Well," Nick said. "They live in the Market. It's not that far to walk." He didn't really like Stephen Baker or Stephen Brooks—the Stephen Bees—very much. They were some of Erik's closest friends, but they were also the ones that didn't often make him feel particularly welcome. Stephen Baker had offered him a glass of milk at one of their wine-tasting parties, ostensibly as a joke, but...

"Like I said." Erik smiled at him, but Nick could see he wasn't interested. "We'll see."

They stared at each other. Nick turned to Fiona. "We could head out right after the countdown. That way we're not running out on the Stephen Bees, but we'll still get to see you guys."

"Great," Fiona said. Then she tilted her head. "The Stephen Bees?"

"Stephen Baker and Stephen Brooks," Nick said. "They're kind of identical, too. Between you and me, it's a bit incestuous."

Fiona laughed, but Erik frowned.

"They're not related. They just look a lot like each other."

"I didn't mean literally," Nick said. "But you gotta admit…"

Erik finally smiled. "You're right."

"I love it when you say those words," Nick said and leaned over to give Erik a kiss. He pressed a hand to Erik's chest, the ornament looped on his finger.

"What's that?" Matt asked.

Nick held it up. "Haruto gave it to me. It's the cover of my first book."

"You're an author?" Johnny asked. "What kind of book is it?"

"Gay romance. He does short stories," Erik said. "He's really good. If he wrote more mainstream stuff, he could make it big."

"I like writing gay characters," Nick said, shrugging.

"That's was really sweet of Haruto," Fiona said.

"Yeah," Erik said. He took the ornament from Nick and looked at it. "Wasn't it?" He leaned back in his chair and managed to get it onto the tree on one of the lower branches. "Maybe this means we could get rid of the old paper crane?"

"Bite your tongue," Nick said. "That thing is sacrosanct. It's where it all began."

"New house, new beginnings," Erik said and wrapped an arm around him, pulling him right onto his lap. Nick loved the way he felt when Erik held him like that. Wanted. He didn't need to be a shrink to know why that was important to him, but it didn't make it feel any less wonderful.

"So who wants to watch *The Muppet Christmas Carol*?" Fiona asked.

Nick groaned into Erik's chest.

"Hey," Erik said. "You invited her."

CHAPTER 5

SIXTH CHRISTMAS

Nick's phone rang. He shifted his bags into one hand, dug it out, saw who was calling, and nearly dropped it trying to answer it as fast as he could.

"Is it the baby?" he asked, breathless. "Are you having the baby?"

"It's not the baby," Fiona said. "Still pregnant. Believe me, no one wants the leech to make her debut more than I do, but I've got three weeks left and she's not showing any signs of being early. I can live with that. Just so long as she isn't late. I feel like warmed-over crap."

"Aw, I bet you're glowing." Nick shifted the bags again, getting a better grip. He balanced his phone against his shoulder.

"I'm not glowing. I'm miserable. That glowing stuff is lies. All lies. I sweat. That's all I do. And pee. Pee and sweat. Which you'd know, by the way, if I'd seen you at all in the last two months."

Nick winced. "I know. I'm a horrible human being. The new store was a mess, and I got there just in time for the shit to hit the fan for Christmas. The previous manager hadn't even hired anyone, so I had to work extra to get the training done and..." He sighed. "Whatever. Who cares? I have staff now and it's going better than it has any right to go. But once Boxing Week is done, I've got a couple of days before we go to Provincetown. Assuming the joyous event hasn't happened yet, we'll definitely get together. I promise."

"Oh. That's right. I forgot about P-Town," Fiona said. "Damn. Well, that screws up that plan."

Nick slowed down. "What's wrong?"

"Have you spoken to Haruto today?"

"No. We got together a couple of weeks ago for coffee," Nick said. "Why? What's wrong?" Haruto and Nick usually managed to sneak in coffee every week or so, but once retail Christmas hit, things had gotten away from Nick. And Erik didn't really like it when what little time he did have off went to other people.

"His father had a heart attack this morning. It wasn't as bad as it could have been, I guess, but he's going to be laid up for a while and needs someone to help him. I just got off the phone with Haruto a few minutes ago, and he's kind of a mess. There's no one else to help out but him, so he has to be the one. He's leaving tomorrow. You know how he feels about Oneida."

"Oh no," Nick said. He sighed. "That's awful."

"I'd kind of wondered if you'd maybe have been able to visit him after Christmas, just to make sure he was okay, but...I forgot P-Town."

"Shit, shit, shit," Nick said.

"That's about the whole of it. Jenn doesn't want to go, because, y'know, *baby*." Fiona paused. "Hey, you're panting. Are *you* okay?"

"I'm having such a shitty day, though now I feel like a selfish ass for saying so. Erik's been in a foul mood for weeks—he's tired of being a retail widow. Would you believe in order to get my shit done I lied through my teeth and said I was working today? This is my last day off before Christmas, and I'm trying to accomplish everything before he comes home from work so I can surprise him with alone time. I drove to Centrum to get the last presents, pick up something nice for dinner, and mail off the damn Christmas cards, which I finally finished writing; only when I got in line at the post office, I realized I left the fucking cards at home. There was no way I was fighting for another parking spot—it took me almost half an hour to find one the first time—and I still have to get the groceries, so I figured it'd be faster to walk home, drop off what I'd done already, pick up the cards, and then walk back to Centrum to get the stamps and mail them."

"You *drove* to Centrum? Isn't that, like, a five-minute walk?"

"It's snowing. I'm grumpy, and I was buying groceries."

Fiona laughed. "No judgement. I'd take a car to the bathroom at this point, if I could."

"Anyway, I'm almost home, but I'm half jogging. That's why I'm doing the heavy breathing."

"Don't worry about it. Anyway, I thought I'd fill you in about Haruto. I just don't want him to be out there alone if we can help it. Hey, maybe I'll see if Phoebe can check in on him."

"Isn't she doing that fashion show thing in Toronto?"

"Of course. Right," Fiona said. "Baby brain is a real thing. I'm barely smart enough to tie my shoes, and that's assuming I can reach the fucking things. Shit! That's a loonie to the swear jar."

"By my count, that's two," Nick said. Jenn was trying to cure Fiona of her swearing habit before the baby arrived. It wasn't working.

"I've only got a five-dollar bill. I'll come up with three more before dinner. I'm sorry your day sucks, and I'm sorry Erik is still a selfish turd."

"Hey, now," Nick said. "That's my man."

"You know your man is a selfish turd sometimes. Good luck with your Christmas cards. Maybe I'll try Matt and Johnny."

"Good idea," Nick said. "Oh, and hey—I really am sorry I haven't seen much of you lately. The new store... Lots of stuff."

"Also my leech. I'm sorry you weren't at the Misfit Toys. You missed a great time."

Nick sighed. His traditional Christmas event had fallen by the wayside for the first time in five years when Erik had put his foot down about the two of them spending time together by themselves at least once in December. Nick had relented, and when the day in question had arrived, Erik had taken him out to one of the most expensive restaurants in the Market, and then Chances, where they'd ended up dancing off their meal on a loud and crowded dance floor. The sex after had been good, though he'd already been tired enough for bed and had really only engaged because Erik had so obviously intended that to be the end of their evening, but the night hadn't honestly included much "together time" otherwise, and Nick had spent the next day at work even more exhausted than usual.

"Shit happens," he said. "There, now you only have two swears left."

"Pay your own way," Fiona said. "I gotta go. I need to pee. Again."

"Okay. I'll call you once Christmas is done."

"You do that."

She hung up. Nick stopped walking long enough to dial Haruto and then started walking again. He was almost home. Haruto picked up on the second ring.

"I take it Fiona called you?"

"She did. How are you doing?"

"My father's going to be okay. He just needs a hand for a bit."

"Yeah, but it means going home," Nick said, knowing full well that Haruto was being falsely upbeat.

"Sure does. Maybe Oneida changed in the last decade."

Nick laughed. "Right."

"Yeah, well. Hey, any chance I can swing round your place tomorrow? I have your present to drop off."

"And I have yours," Nick said. "But I'll be at work doing a double. Erik will be home after five." He turned the corner and frowned. Erik's car was in the driveway. He shouldn't have been home yet—he hoped nothing had gone wrong at the gym. The last thing he needed was another run-in with Erik in a foul mood. He couldn't wait to get to Provincetown, even in January. They needed to reconnect. At least he didn't have to fish out his keys.

"Good. I'll drop it off. You're going to love this year's ornament."

"Is it another hunky merman?" Last year Nick had ended up with a merman in a leather harness.

"You'll have to wait and see."

Nick opened the front door and stepped inside. He froze.

Haruto was talking again, but Nick didn't hear it. He stared down. The black leather jacket, and the expensive Marmot boots, and the cherry-red scarf made sense, though it wasn't like Erik to toss his clothes on

the floor like that—he liked the house tidy and orga-
nized and usually hung everything up. But the other
coat, and the other boots, and the second scarf?

Those Nick didn't recognize.

Except. Except maybe he did.

"Nick?" Haruto's voice sounded concerned. Nick
snapped out of it.

"I'll call you back," Nick said quietly and hung up. He
stopped, standing in the entrance hall, listening. Was
that a murmur? He wasn't sure. Nick didn't bother taking off his own boots, leaving a wet trail of snow across
the entrance hall and past the living room and kitchen
to the stairs. There he saw Erik's black tank top tossed
to the side of the stairs, along with a red soccer shirt.

Nick looked up the stairs, deciding. For longer than
he liked, he considered turning around, getting the
Christmas cards from the dining room table, and leaving. He could mail the cards. Come back home when he
was supposed to come home from his day at "work." He
could...

What? Forget it? Pretend I have no idea?

He closed his eyes, his chest tight.

I've already been doing that.

He opened his eyes. His Christmas tree was there in
the living room. Decorated with one of Erik's
themes—antique gold and silver—his own eclectic ornaments had been tucked aside this year in favour of a
stylish tree. At the time, Nick had decided it hadn't
bothered him much and was pleased when Erik had

suggested they compromise by filling up empty branches with candy canes. It looked polished and beautiful, like it belonged in a magazine.

It was very Erik. Like the whole house. Like the vacation. Like the boots and jacket and scarf and...

Nick took a deep breath and started up the stairs, moving as quietly as he could manage in his boots. Not that he needed to bother. The closer he got, the more the murmurs were revealed as moans. Nick knew those noises. He'd been the source of some of them, as recently as that last dinner out. When he got to the bedroom door, which was open, Nick leaned in the doorway, seeing more than enough in the first few seconds. Erik was on top, of course, and the young man writhing under him was definitely the guy he remembered seeing in the coat downstairs. He worked for Erik at the gym.

Among other things, apparently.

"Ho, ho, *fucking* ho," Nick said loudly. "Literally."

SEVENTH CHRISTMAS

———————

"Hey," Nick said. "I'm sorry to do this on so little no-tice; it's just I can't find them, and if it turns out they were left at Erik's, then..." He shook his head. "I really hope he wouldn't have thrown them out if they were."

"It's fine," Jenn said. Her hair was covered in a scarf, and she had Melody on one hip, but she smiled and stepped to the side to let him in.

Nick pulled off his boots and coat, tucking them neatly aside in the small entrance hall. Fiona and Jenn's townhouse was a long and narrow affair, and de-spite his rising panic, he smiled at the sight of the Christmas decorations that seemed to have exploded onto every wall.

"Wow," he said. "You guys are in the spirit."

"It's all Fiona," Jenn said.

"You're *kidding*."

"I think she wants Melody's first Christmas to be

perfect. Kind of like the ones she never had." Jenn said. "Can you believe yesterday we were baking Christmas cookies that Melody can eat? They're sugar-free, peanut-free, and if you ask me they taste like butt, but Melody seems to love them."

Nick smiled. "You look wonderful."

Jenn laughed. "Only a gay white boy would look at this and say 'wonderful.' Melody woke up three times last night, this is yesterday's shirt, and I haven't even looked at my hair yet today. I'm sure there's a word for how I look, but it's not 'wonderful.'"

Nick shook his head. "Fine. How about 'happy'? You look happy."

Jenn nodded. "That's because we are; aren't we, El-ladee?" She nestled her nose in Melody's hair and took a sniff. When she saw Nick blink, she shrugged. "She smells good. It's a thing."

"I'll take your word for it."

"C'mon," Jenn said. "Sniff the child. All the cool kids do it."

"I'm good." Nick held up one hand.

"Ba," Melody said, waving one chubby hand.

"No, I'm Nick. Nick," Nick said, tapping his chest.

"If she says your name before Mama, you realize Fiona will murder you."

"I can dream."

"Come on through. Melody should be going down for a nap now—if there's really a God—and then I can help you look through your boxes."

"I swear I will come and get them," Nick said. "As soon as I find a better place."

"And I know Fiona has told you we don't mind, so I won't repeat it. It's not a lot, and it's not like we're using the basement for anything. Maybe one day we'll finish it…" She exhaled. "Okay, missy. Time for bed."

Nick watched Jenn take Melody up the narrow stairs and marvelled at the room while she was gone. Paper snowflakes. Santas. Red construction paper with white baby handprints and footprints decorated as reindeer or snowmen or… Nick wasn't sure what some of the blobs were supposed to be, but they were probably festive nonetheless. What was it Haruto always said? Hand-made gifts had heart. There was a lot of heart here. It was hard to picture Fiona this way—happy for the season, excited to be sharing it with her family. Then again, she was the last person he'd ever expected to have a baby. But here she was, with Jenn and their daughter. And if things went the way they seemed to be going, they might even be allowed to get married.

His smile faded a little. He was happy for her; he really was. And just a little bit sad and jealous and…

"You okay?" Jenn asked. She had returned without Melody. She'd pulled her long brown hair into a messy bun and was carrying a baby monitor.

"I'm good," Nick said. And he meant it, mostly.

They went into the basement and found the stacks of boxes that Nick had moved into their home a year earlier. Most were unlabelled. It had been a horrible couple of days, and not made much better by the dawning realization that Nick hadn't owned very much after all. So much of what had been his had been tossed or donated because Erik's belongings had been better than his. He hadn't even owned a frying pan. Most of what was in the boxes had been books, clothes, and other random bits and pieces that he'd scoured from Erik's house. He'd been lucky. Matt and Johnny had helped him, and Erik—beyond the initial ugly explosion—had left them to it.

As he looked at the boxes now, everything felt fresh again.

"He was an asshole," Jenn said.

Nick smiled. "Some days I remember he wasn't all bad, but I'm firmly in 'asshole' camp today, so I agree."

They started opening boxes. The first two were books, of course, and Nick had to fight the urge to rescue some comfort reads to take back to his already stuffed apartment. He didn't have room, and he had more than enough books back home. This was a specific mission.

He did find one of his writing journals that he'd been searching out for ages, a notebook in which he'd scribbled plot ideas. Why it was mixed in with some towels and a bath mat he wasn't sure, though he supposed he did get a lot of ideas while he soaked in the bathtub. He tucked it aside and moved on.

"Found them," Jenn said.

Nick exhaled, relief flooding through him. She was

standing by the other end of where his boxes were stacked, having already looked through her third or fourth box. He went to her and looked down.

"Oh, thank God," he said.

They'd been packed in with some of the extra copies of the first two anthologies he'd been published in and padded with a Christmas stocking and the strings of tinsel. He saw the rainbow unicorn kitten and one of Haruto's tacky butch-gay mermaids and felt tears sting his eyes.

"Hey," Jenn said, stroking his shoulder. "It's okay. We found them."

He nodded. "I know. It's dumb. I shouldn't be upset."

"Of course you should," Jenn said. "This is your version of Melody's first Christmas. I wasn't there when it started, but Fiona told me. You guys made something for yourselves. That's important."

"Well," Nick said. "No party this year, either." Johnny and Matt were hosting Johnny's grandmother's visit now that they'd moved in together, Fiona and Jenn were obviously less mobile these days, and he hadn't seen Haruto in months. He'd been living in Oneida since his father's second heart attack.

Nick needed to call him.

"You want to join us for ours? Phoebe is coming, and she's bringing Morgan and Zach. And my mother will be here, so there's likely to be off-key singing." Jenn wagged her eyebrows. "*Loud,* off-key singing of traditional Christmas songs. She does an incredible 'Round and Round the Christmas Tree.' It's practically atonal. Come on. How can you say no?"

"As delightful as that sounds, I get enough Christmas carols at work," Nick said. "But actually, if you're sure it wouldn't be an imposition, I would love to drop by for a bit Christmas Day. Just for a little while."

"Of course you can. No one can resist my mother's singing," Jenn said.

"Does she do 'Baby, It's Cold Outside'?" Nick asked. "Maybe I'll duet with her."

Jenn narrowed her eyes. "Don't make me uninvite you."

Nick laughed and lifted the box. "Thanks for helping me."

"Any time. You need a hand with it?"

Nick shook his head. "I'm good."

He took the box to his car and made good time back to his apartment for a change. Once he was home, he put the box on his small kitchen table and opened it again. The Christmas tree was already up, the misshapen box left in the middle of the floor from when he'd realized he had no idea where the ornaments were. He had gone through the two closets in his apartment with mounting panic before he'd called Jenn to ask her if he could come over and check what was still stored in their basement.

He pulled out the tinsel carefully and wrapped it around the tree. He wanted to feel better about this, his first Christmas in his new apartment. But the reality was it was just reminding him about last year's horrible mix of retail and breakup. He hadn't even had time to breathe, let alone mourn, and when Erik had taken his new boyfriend with him to Provincetown on what was supposed to have been *their* post-Christmas vacation, he'd nearly lost it. At least the time had been booked off already. Phoebe had helped him find a new apartment, and Matt and Johnny had helped him move what he'd needed over, while Morgan had been an angel and taken the rest of the boxes to Fiona's basement. He'd ended up visiting Haruto after all, which had been the only bright thing about the entire episode.

Tinsel finished, Nick looked in the box and smiled grimly when he saw the blue paper crane.

"And here we are again," Nick said, putting it on the tree, front and centre. "Back in a small apartment, by ourselves, ready for another *awesome* holiday season." He rolled his eyes, annoyed at his own mood. Besides, it wasn't true. He wasn't alone. Okay, yes, he was single—*again*—and yes, there was no party this year—*again*—but this wasn't a crappy bachelor apartment. He was the manager of the second largest Book It in the province, and he was a twice-published author, albeit of gay short stories in anthologies almost no one had read. This wasn't starting over. Not really. He looked in the box again, picked up the rainbow kitten unicorn ornament, and grinned. The rivalry between him and Matt for the kitten had been epic, but Nick had been the last number drawn out of the deck that year. He put it on the tree. Then he hung a white-lace snowflake. Haruto's tacky merman was up next, and he followed that up with the ceramic book cover. When he'd hung all the ornaments, he stepped back, looking at the tree a long while. It was by no means full—he'd fill it in with candy canes, of course—but every ornament there made it clear: this wasn't starting over.

He had an idea. He glanced around and found the journal he'd rediscovered in Jenn's basement and flipped it open to an empty page. He grabbed a pen and sat cross-legged in front of the tree, writing the idea down before it could flee the way ideas always seemed to, when he had them in the shower, or while he was driving to work. He closed the journal and smiled up at the tree again. His gaze caught on the blue paper crane, and he pulled out his phone.

Haruto picked up on the second ring.

"Hello?"

"Hey, you," Nick said. "I just put your crane on the tree. And your tacky merman. And that beautiful one you had made for me, the one with the book cover."

"Aw," Haruto said. "Has someone been getting maudlin?"

"Great word. I should use that in a story."

"If you do, I want half the profits."

"I don't know. Twenty-five bucks can change a man."

"At this point, I'd just rather it could buy me a man. Even for an hour."

"Ouch," Nick said. "Rough time in Oneida?"

"It's as charming as ever. But! I've actually been chatting with someone online who lives in the middle of nowhere, which is like half an hour from here."

"You naughty minx. Are you *sexting*?"

"Please. I wish. He's a farmer, if you can imagine. We've been discussing the various merits of being queer and living in a small town. My list was shorter than his."

"He has merits?"

"*He* has plenty. He's handsome, in a Farmer Bob way, if I can believe his profile image. But the small town thing? You know how I feel about that."

Nick laughed. "I believe you've made yourself clear. How's your dad?"

"Unstoppable. I caught him sneaking bacon again. I can't blame him. If someone told me it was bacon or a heart attack, I'd seriously consider bacon." He paused. "But, honestly, he's doing a little better. He's not a young guy. He hates not being able to be as active as he used to be. He misses his walks, and he still makes me drop him by his school when I go grocery shopping—his students love him, though I'm not sure the principal loves how he disrupts everything—but mostly he sits and reads or watches television. He falls asleep sometimes while we're playing Scrabble. It's a little sad."

"I'm sorry."

"It is what it is. How about you? Any hot dates on the horizon?"

"I'm going to sing with Jenn's mother on Christmas

Day. I plan to convince her to sing 'Baby, It's Cold Out-side.'"

"You're a monster." Haruto laughed. Nick's chest ached at the sound. He hadn't realized just how much he was missing Haruto.

"Ten bucks says Fiona has to fill the swear jar," Nick said.

"No bet."

"I miss you," Nick said.

"Aw, maudlin Nick is maudlin."

They sat in silence for a moment.

"Any new stories in the pipeline?" Haruto asked. "You know I need me some more Nicholas Wilson for my bookshelf. Also, it's really easy to buy you a present if I just have to have an ornament made to match the book cover. The second one is in the mail, by the way."

"That's awesome. I love them. As for new stories, numbers three and four are in production, and I sent off a fifth and a sixth last month. I've not been writing much the last two months; it's too busy, but with a little luck, you might end up with four new books before next year is done."

"That's fantastic. And a novel?"

"Funny man. I write short stories."

"Don't think you can get away with that excuse for-ever, mister. I am too fabulous to be denied."

"I'm sure Farmer Bob agrees."

"Kevin. It's Farmer Kevin."

"Well, Farmer Kevin, then," Nick said. Then, with a

strange little twist in his stomach, he asked, "You going to meet up with him?"

"Is it terrible if I say yes?"

"Of course not," Nick said, though the twist grew a little tighter. "You deserve some happiness, mister."

"That's just it. I wonder if he's doing the same thing I'm doing. It's not like we're spoiled for choice, right? I mean, don't get me wrong, at least his profile isn't all 'no fats, no fems, no Asians' like Erik's was, but—"

"Whoa," Nick said. "Pardon?"

Silence.

"Ru?" Nick asked.

"Sorry," Haruto said, and Nick could imagine the cringe on Haruto's face. "Damn it. I wasn't ever going to say anything about that."

"Please do," Nick said.

"There's not a whole lot to say. It's just, when Fiona first introduced us, I realized I'd seen him from somewhere before. I'd read his online profile and had been impressed he was a big reader, because let's be honest, he didn't really look like one. He looked like a big dumb jock. And I was tempted to send him a message, right up until I got to the end of his profile and saw it. 'No fats, no fems...'"

"'No Asians,'" they said together.

"Yeah."

"I'm so sorry," Nick said.

"Why? You didn't write it."

"No, but I *dated* it. I had no idea. I never saw his profile, I swear." But Nick had definitely seen the way he treated Haruto, and Johnny, who could sometimes camp it up with the best of them. Erik couldn't abide feminine guys. Not to mention how he'd treated Phoebe. Erik wasn't just a misogynist, he was a transphobe, and Nick hated how he'd barely spoken up, convincing himself he could "teach" Erik to be more open-minded despite all the evidence to the contrary, and generally letting himself get too caught up in feeling good about having someone who wanted him around. Until he didn't. "I'm really sorry. He was always such a shit to you guys."

"Well," Haruto said. "We live and we learn. Maybe Farmer Kevin will be more open-minded."

"I hope so. Because you, sir, are fabulous. And hot."

"Babe, I know it." Haruto laughed. "I need to go. I haven't started making dinner yet, and I promised soba noodles."

"Listen, post-Christmas, I will find time to visit."

"We can meet halfway and do coffee," Haruto said. "No reason for you to come all this way. Besides, Pickering at least has a Starbucks."

"Okay. Merry Christmas, Ru."

"Merry Christmas, Nicky."

Nick hung up.

CHAPTER

7

NINTH CHRISTMAS

"Oh my God, look at you," Nick said.

Haruto's hair was artfully arranged in a series of little spikes, each tip dyed a deep blue. He had new glasses, too, rimless and very sleek. He wore a black pea coat, a teal scarf, and skinny jeans that showed off his trim waist and long legs. He looked fantastic. Even the designer black leather messenger bag he was carrying was chic.

"Thank you, thank you." Haruto raised his hands and did a little twirl and then sat down across from him. "I may be in the sticks, and I might be on the doorstep of the big three-oh, but I don't have to announce it. The Internet delivers everywhere."

Their usual coffee shop in Pickering had been their meeting place for the last couple of years and was their springboard for the day's shopping. They both intended to polish off their Christmas lists today, have dinner together, and then Nick would make the drive back. The last week until Christmas was almost on him, and the bookstore had been ramping up insanely over the last couple of weeks. He could almost taste his third-quarter bonus and intended to pre-spend a lot of it today.

"Love the hair," Nick said.

"Thank you. I finally found a decent hair stylist within a three-hour radius. Kevin thinks it's a bit much, but his idea of style is a bit more pastoral than mine." He looked at Nick, one eyebrow creeping up. "So. Your hair. If you like, I can give you her name."

"Nice. Very nice. For this, I drove through a blizzard?" Nick said.

"It's barely flurries," Haruto said.

Nick smiled. "You tell Kevin from me that your hair is fabulous. We city folk know our stuff."

"I will. He's just not up on things like hair styles or clothes or music," Haruto said. He took a sip from his latte and let out a long, low moan. "Or real, honest-to-God, magic coffee."

"Are we sure he's gay?" Nick asked.

"Oh, he's very much gay," Haruto said. "In all the ways that really matter." He winked.

"TMI." Nick laughed and tried not to squirm. He was glad to see Haruto look happier, though at the same time, he felt the sting of missing his best friend.

"Well, we're finding middle ground outside the bedroom," Haruto said. "I have even milked a cow. And that's not a euphemism."

Nick whistled. "That's just not something I ever thought I'd hear you say."

"You're telling me," Haruto said. "Now, give me the gossip."

"You speak to everyone more than I do, I think," Nick said. "I'm buried in Christmas retail."

"Text messages and Facebook are not the same. Tell me." He picked up his coffee and took another long pull.

"Um, okay. Phoebe has finally gotten onto the waiting list for surgery. That's pretty huge news, and I think she and Dennis are dating now, though she's being coy about it."

"Is Dennis the hunky bisexual bear bartender?"

"I'm not sure I'd call him a bear. I think he prefers 'otter.' But yeah, he's got a pretty impressive beard."

"Bear makes for better alliteration. Otter, hipster, lumberjack, whatever. I'm not one to throw stones." Haruto smiled over his cup. "He better treat Phoebe right."

"I think he knows we'll kill him if he doesn't."

"Good."

"Oh, and Melody is apparently very much *not* pleased that she'll be getting a baby brother sometime next summer. Jenn and Fiona are working the 'you get to be the older sister' angle."

"I still can't believe they're spawning again."

"Is it really *spawning* when you import frozen sperm?" Nick asked.

Haruto tilted his head. "Point. How's Jenn handling being pregnant?"

"Better than Fiona is handling Jenn being pregnant, that's for sure. Jenn has forbidden her from going online and looking up pregnancy symptoms. Never mind that Fiona got through it all herself; suddenly Jenn is the most fragile creature in all of creation."

"That's sort of sweet," Haruto said. "And how are the boys?"

"Away. Morgan and Zach went skiing. Johnny and Matt send their love, and they said if they get to meet Celine in person, they will get her autograph for you."

Haruto narrowed his eyes. "Bitches. Had to rub that in one more time, eh?"

"I don't think they'll meet her. It's just a concert cruise." Nick shrugged. "Celine's not all that."

"You did not just say that about Celine." Haruto leaned back.

"I surrender," Nick said, though he smiled. "Don't flog me."

"You'd love it too much," Haruto said. He tipped his cup back, draining the last of the coffee. "Before we go…" He reached down to his messenger bag and pulled out a small, wrapped package. He slid it across the table.

Nick grinned. "Aww." He held up his hand. "I have one for you, too." He lifted a gift bag from beneath the table and passed it to Haruto. Haruto clapped his hands and tore at the tissue.

"Oh. My. God," Haruto said. He pulled out the first

can of gourmet coffee. There were five more in the bag.

"They're all from Bittersweets," Nick said and held up his hand before Haruto could interrupt him. "And yes, the one in the Village, not the one in the Market."

"Their grinder is better."

"Of course it is," Nick said, carefully undoing the tape on his own small package. When he pulled off the paper and opened the box, he froze.

It was a ceramic ornament, and it was the cover of a book. *The* book. There was his name, and the art-work—a handsome man facing something just out of sight. The whole image was soft and muted, giving it a faded, almost dreamy quality. The artwork was gor-geous, but it wasn't possible, because... He stared at Haruto, his mouth open.

"So *maybe* I got in touch with your publisher and begged, wheedled, and pleaded for the cover art for your collection. I didn't get to design it—though thanks to you, they're going to put me on the freelance list—so if you hate it, don't blame me, but I think it's great." He smiled. "I explained your whole ornament tradition to your editor, Stacia. I had her nearly in tears. Lovely girl, by the way. Anyway, she sent me the file, I had it made, and *surprise*! This is what your very first collected vol-ume of short fiction is going to look like, Famous Au-thor Nicholas Wilson." He leaned forward and grinned conspiratorially. "I even asked them to tell you the final artwork was delayed so you wouldn't be able to see it before you got this."

It was true. His publisher had told him there was a slight delay with the artwork, but that it wouldn't affect the release date. Lying liars.

"I can't decide whether to hug you or smack you right now."

"I will settle for you picking up the check for dinner," Haruto said.

Nick looked back at the ornament. His eyes were wet.

"And don't think this lets you off the hook," Haruto said. "I still want a novel, mister."

"I write short stories," Nick said.

"Uh-huh," Haruto said. "Come on. Let's go single-handedly rescue capitalism."

TENTH CHRISTMAS

Nick came to in inches, fighting through waves of nausea and a sluggishness that lay over him like piles of blankets. He wanted to wake up and wanted to sit up, but everything seemed more difficult than it should have been.

His mouth tasted awful. That was the first thing. He wanted some water or to brush his teeth. And his gut ached in an awful, distant way.

He frowned, grunted, and finally opened his eyes. They felt gritty and gross. He raised his hand to wipe them, and an arc of dull pain moved through his abdomen.

"Ow," he said. He blinked a few more times, wiped his eyes, and rolled his head to the side.

Where am I?

He didn't recognize the room. It was plain and white,

and he was staring at a wall with a convoluted shelf and swing-out table and...

Hospital.

It came back to him. He'd been at Book It, halfway through a shift, working the lines and the front half of the store. It had been a great day, and really busy, and if his stomachache hadn't been going away, that was just retail during the holidays for you. He'd swallowed some antacid and some painkillers on his break, and that had been fine. Except he'd just shown someone where this year's *Guinness Book of World Records* had been stacked when the stomachache had gone beyond ache and into pain. And then from pain into outright agony.

Had he fallen down?

"Hello?" he said.

"Well hello, sunshine."

Nick rolled his head in the other direction. There were two chairs in the room, and on one of them sat Phoebe. She folded the corner of the page in her book and closed it.

"Hi," Nick said. He still felt confused, and his throat was sore. He coughed. "Is there water?"

Phoebe nodded, rose, and moved to the small table beside the bed that Nick hadn't noticed. She picked up a cup and leaned over him. He went to take it from her but groaned when he tried to shift.

"Don't try to sit up. You had surgery."

He widened his eyes but waited until after he took a couple of sips of water—he felt pathetic, having Phoebe tip the glass to his lips, but right now he just wanted to drink something—to try to speak again.

"Surgery?"

"You know that stomach bug you were telling us about?" Phoebe said.

He nodded.

"Appendicitis." She put the cup down. "You. Are. An. Idiot."

"Did I pass out at the store?" Nick said. "I don't really remember."

"You did." She turned back to him, and he saw she was crying.

"Hey," he said. "Don't."

"Your appendix burst," she said. "People still die from that, you know."

He took a breath. It didn't hurt too much. He realized he was probably on painkillers and looked at his left hand. There was an IV. "I'm sorry. I honestly thought it was just a stomach bug or something. It's our busy time, and I didn't want to take a sick day…"

"Yeah, well," Phoebe said. "It wasn't a stomach bug. And that goddamn bookstore will have to go on without you for a while."

"Oh crap, the store…" he said, but the glower Phoebe aimed his way made him reconsider. "Will be fine without me," he said carefully.

She nodded. "Yes. It will. Now, apparently you're in here for at least another night or two, but after that, you're going to stay with Matt and Johnny."

He opened his mouth, but Phoebe raised her hand. "No arguments."

He closed his mouth.

The door opened. Nick turned his head, and despite feeling like utter crap, he smiled.

"You are an *idiot*," Haruto said, once he saw Nick was awake.

"We covered that," Phoebe said.

"Hey, Ru," Nick said. "I'm sorry."

"You're sprung," Haruto said to Phoebe. He put a small gym bag down between the two chairs and aimed a thumb at the door. "Go home."

Phoebe rose and stretched. "Gladly. These chairs are shitty."

"Loonie in the jar," Nick and Haruto said in tandem. They looked at each other and grinned.

"Fiona and Jenn aren't here," Phoebe said. "And neither is Melody. So... Fuckity-fuck, fuck-fuck-fuck." She pulled on her coat, hugged Haruto, and then looked down at Nick.

"Feel better," she said. "And let us know if you need anything."

"Don't yell at me, but the only thing I think I need is to let work know what's going on," Nick said. "My regional manager, at the very least."

"Once you were out of surgery I called the store and told them," Phoebe said. "I also told them you might not be able to get in touch with them for a couple of days, which I'd like you to take not as a suggestion but as an order."

"How about I just hang on to this?" Haruto said, and Nick looked over just in time to see him pocket Nick's phone.

"I surrender," Nick said.

"Good." Phoebe squeezed his shoulder and then leaned in and kissed his forehead. "Look, sweetie, I get it. I run my own shop, too, remember? But your health? More important."

She wrapped a gorgeous red shawl over her shoulders.

"One of yours?" Nick said.

"Phoebe original," she said. A moment later, she was gone.

"God, I miss her," Haruto said.

"When did you get here?" Nick asked.

"Kevin drove me down while you were getting sliced up."

Nick shifted a little on the bed, but nothing felt quite comfortable.

"The buttons are here," Haruto said, pointing to the side of the bed. Nick nodded and pressed the one that would raise his head a bit. It felt better to be more upright, though he wondered how long that would last.

"Is Kevin here, too?" he asked.

"No, he's looking after my dad until I go back."

"How's your dad?" Nick asked.

Haruto sighed. "Honestly? Not good." He sat down in

the chair Phoebe had vacated and leaned back. "Is it terrible that coming here to sit with you feels like an escape? It is, isn't it? I'm a terrible person."

"Worse than Satan," Nick said.

Haruto narrowed his eyes. "Keep that up and no presents."

Nick laughed and then winced. "Ow. Okay, I think whatever they gave me for the pain is wearing off."

"Hrm." Haruto reached down and picked up the gym bag. "I took your keys and went back to your place. I brought your robe, and your pyjama bottoms—by the way, you need better pyjamas—and a couple of books from your beside table. Toothbrush, deodorant, all the basics."

"Bless you," Nick said.

"And..." Haruto put his hand in his pocket and pulled out something that had been hastily covered in tissue paper. "It turns out there's a gift shop downstairs for the truly desperate." He passed it to Nick, who carefully moved his left hand to hold it—he didn't want to tug on the IV—and then peeled off the tissue with his right.

It was an ornament, of course. A snowman doctor. He had a stethoscope, a white jacket, and a little clipboard with a prescription symbol on it.

"Thank you. I love him." Nick held the little snowman up. "Now I'll never forget this magical time."

Haruto snorted. "Well, just so we're clear, the moment you fall asleep again I'm heading for the nearest coffee shop."

"Of course. When's Kevin coming back for you?"

"He can handle Dad for today, tonight, and tomorrow, but then he's going to come get me tomorrow night. We'll sleep over at Phoebe's and then head back out first thing. Kevin's sister said she'd stay with my dad until we got back."

"You didn't have to come," Nick said. "I'm really glad to see you, but you didn't have to screw up everyone's schedule like that."

"Pft," Haruto said. "Like I said. This is an escape."

Nick reached out and squeezed his hand. Haruto regarded him for a long moment.

"You scared everybody," he said.

Nick nodded. "Didn't mean to."

"Well, no more skipped coffee dates, mister. We'll make it work. And what's this I hear about not even having a Misfits party this year?"

Nick sighed. "Work was too busy, and I wasn't feeling all that great…"

"Because you're an idiot."

"Because I'm an idiot. Well established. Y'know, I think you missed your calling as a nurse. You overflow with empathy."

Haruto shook his head. "No, I don't. Just ask my father."

Nick winced. "Sorry. I didn't mean that."

Haruto sighed. "Okay. Enough about all that. How's about we gossip instead? Phoebe was here alone. I need intel before I get there. Is Dennis on the outs?"

Nick relaxed back into his pillow and raised one finger. "That depends on who you ask."

TWELFTH CHRISTMAS

"Hey, you." Nick opened his arms.

Haruto took one look at Nick, tried a smile, and then all but threw himself into the hug. Nick squeezed him and rubbed his back, feeling him tremble. Nick glanced around the coffee shop. They'd gotten the attention of the barista and a couple of the customers, but nothing looked hostile or worrisome.

"Sorry," Haruto said, after he'd gathered himself for a couple of seconds. They broke apart slowly, Haruto wiping his eyes with his chartreuse scarf before meeting Nick's gaze again. "Apparently, I'm still a bit weepy."

"Of course you are," Nick said. He nodded to the table where Haruto had been sitting, and they both sat down.

Haruto took a long breath and picked up his latte, holding it between his hands like he was trying to draw on the warmth in the cup.

"What do you need?" Nick asked. "Help with the funeral? If there's anything I can do, just let me know."

"The funeral's the easy part," Haruto said. "My father, the planner. He already paid for his cremation, bought a little cubby thing for his ashes... Even the music for the memorial was all planned out." He leaned forward. "Between you and me, I think he was afraid I'd do something too extravagant for his tastes. Like I'd hire a clown or something."

Nick smiled, though he saw right through Haruto's flippancy.

"You know, it's okay to be relieved," Nick said.

Haruto glanced down at the table, still holding his cup. "Thank you." He looked back up again, and there was a tear running down his cheek. "I don't know how you do it, but somehow you always seem to know just what I need to hear." He exhaled. "Last night was the first night I think I've slept through the night in, God, I don't know. Ten months? A year? No little bell ringing. No pills. No bedpan. I woke up this morning, and I stretched and thought, *That was so nice.*" He grimaced. "And then I felt like shit."

Nick reached across the table and squeezed his hand. Haruto shrugged.

"Anyway. Memorial this weekend. I have a shit ton of paperwork to look through. Dad may have planned for everything, but I need to go over it all with his lawyer. I talked to my mom, and there are a few things she'd like, which is nice." He shook his head. "I'm not sure this feels real yet."

"I can't imagine," Nick said.

Haruto groaned. "I'm so sorry. I didn't mean..."

Nick squeezed his hand again. "Oh, my God, no. It's fine. I just meant I couldn't imagine what it would be like to lose someone I'm that close to. My parents weren't that great to begin with and you know that. I don't miss them. I have no idea how they're doing; they've never reached out to me, and most of the time? I'm okay with that." He put his hands on the table. "And it doesn't matter. I'm here for you. Whatever you need."

"What about the store?" Haruto asked. "How did you even score the time off?"

"I have the rest of the week, right through to the end of the weekend. I told my regional what was going on, and he understood. You're my family. You guys dropped everything for me when I was sick." He smiled. "Besides, what was his other option? Not be supportive and fire me? Then he's stuck without a manager three weeks before Christmas. I always overhire to cover for last-minute sick shifts, and the seasonal staff were happy for more hours. I'm good. Don't worry about me."

"Someone has to," Haruto said, and for just a mo-ment, Nick caught that little bit of the old shine. Relief flooded through him.

"So. What can I do?"

Haruto took another deep breath. "Honestly? You

can help me pack. I can't live in that house. I don't want it... I'm selling it."

"Okay," Nick said. He didn't know if it was a fantastic idea to decide something that important right in the moment, but for now, Haruto needed support. "Moving in with Kevin, I'm guessing?"

"That's what he'd like," Haruto said and looked down again.

Nick waited a moment, fighting very hard to keep his voice even. "But?"

"I never wanted to come back to Oneida in the first place. You know that. I've spent five years designing book covers and websites and even pamphlets for local businesses, and okay, yeah, I have some online clients from around the world, and—sure—I've done well for myself, but there's not much more I can do way out there." He sighed. "I miss the city. I miss Bittersweets. I miss the Village, and you and Matt and Fiona and Phoebe and..." He shrugged. "With my dad gone, the only thing keeping me in Oneida is Kevin."

Nick looked at Haruto, *really* looked. His haircut was plain, a simple and manageable style. It flattered him, sure, but it wasn't Haruto. His shirt was a nice shade of blue, yes, but it was just that: a blue button-down shirt.

"You don't feel like you, do you?"

"You're doing it again," Haruto said, but he nodded. "Right. I'm not *me* here. I was for a while...maybe...at the start. But...Kevin is sweet. He's warm and comfortable, and I like how easy it is with him, and oh God, I'm a *horrible* human being."

"Would Kevin come with you?" Nick asked. He realized with no small surprise that the last thing in the world he wanted was for Kevin to move to Ottawa. Haruto, yes. He desperately wanted his Ru back. But Kevin? A rush of something unpleasant—*possessiveness?*—tightened his stomach.

Haruto shook his head. "No. We've talked about it a few times, especially after my father's last stroke. He's a farmer. He always has been, never claimed to be anything else. I'm the one with the business that doesn't need a location."

"That's not entirely true."

Haruto nodded. "I know. But of the two of us?"

"Fair enough," Nick said.

They sat in silence for a while.

"So," Haruto said.

"So."

"We can try the long-distance thing, if he's up for it. It's not like we often got to spend the night with each other unless he came to visit me at Dad's anyway," Haruto said. "Maybe it'll work, right?"

Nick nodded. "It could."

"I'll talk to him before the memorial. I need to tell him I'm not staying. It wouldn't be fair to use him to get through the memorial, just to take off after."

Nick bit his bottom lip. "I'm really sorry."

Haruto leaned back in his chair. "Me too."

"You want another latte?" Nick asked.

"I want a dozen of them," Haruto said. "But I'll take one. To go. C'mon. The sooner we leave, the sooner this week ends."

They rose. Haruto shrugged into his coat and put his scarf back in place. He stopped, looking at Nick. "Did you already have the Misfit Toys party?"

"Nope," Nick said. "It was going to be next Sunday, but obviously, we all delayed. We're planning for the week after next."

Haruto smiled. "I'll be there. My dad has..." He paused, swallowing. "*Had.* My dad had this really pretty set of traditional blown-glass ornaments. If it's okay, I'll bring them and divvy them out. I'm not one for the traditional look, but I think I'd like it if they were scattered about. Y'know, keep them in the family."

"That sounds wonderful," Nick said. He'd make sure he kept some aside, just in case Haruto changed his mind later about the traditional look.

"Good," Haruto said. "Okay. One low-fat mocha latte and we're out of here." He turned to walk to the counter, and Nick followed. While Haruto ordered, Nick pulled out his phone and sent a group text.

I'm here. I think he's going to be fine. He wants to come home.

He hit send and then stepped up to order his own coffee. When he joined Haruto at the bar, while the barista worked on Haruto's latte, his phone pinged. It was Phoebe.

About goddamn time.

A moment later, another ping. Johnny.

If he needs it, spare room is all his.

Ping. Phoebe again.

He's staying with us. Back off, bitches.

Fiona chimed in next. *Christmas Day at our place, then? Melody will lose her shit if Uncle Ru comes to visit.*

"What are you smiling at?" Haruto asked. He held up the two cups.

Nick put his phone away. "The Misfits send their love."

THIRTEEN CHRISTMAS

"Where would you like to put the snowflake?" Nick asked.

"It's pretty," Melody said. She looked at the tree and bit her bottom lip like this was the single most important decision she would ever make. Nick reflected that decorating the tree with Melody might take roughly seven more hours or so.

"It would be best there," she finally said, pointing. Not for the first time, Nick caught a hint of Fiona in her manner. She had a way of stating her opinion that sounded a whole lot like a declaration of fact.

"Got it," Nick said, reaching high up into the tree to put the snowflake on one of the top branches. "Maybe Uncle Ru can pick the next one?" he asked. The two men had offered to babysit for Jenn and Fiona while they got the last of their Christmas shopping done.

"No, I should do it," Melody said, shaking her head.

The responsibility obviously weighed heavily on the shoulders of the five-year-old. Almost six, he reminded himself, and then wondered where he'd put the books he'd brought for her birthday. The hall closet? Maybe. He'd pass them off to Fiona and Jenn when they came back for Melody and Reed.

"I'm fine," Haruto said. He was sitting on the couch with a coffee in one hand and a very sleepy Reed leaning against him. The poor boy was getting over a cold, his moms had warned them, and would probably be super-cranky or crash out. He was well on his way to crashing out but had lived up to the cranky part first, wailing after his sister chose an ornament from the box that he'd wanted to put on the tree. They'd calmed him down, and he was now barely keeping his eyes open while Haruto made up stories for him about a rainbow unicorn kitten named Matthew.

Reed still gripped the ornament in one fist. He'd refused to give it up. Frankly, if it meant he'd sit quietly and get some rest, Nick was fine with him taking it home.

"You sure you're fine?" Nick said.

"No, I'm good here with little Reed."

"I meant more the whole Kevin thing, not the ornaments."

Haruto shrugged. "Kevin deserves a cowboy or something. Or at least someone who doesn't actively dislike animals. He's a good guy. But if I'm honest with myself, he was never *my* good guy."

"Did you break up with Uncle Kevin?" Melody asked.

Nick winced. Right. Melody listened to everything they said.

"Yes, honey. But we're still friends."

Melody frowned. "Do I still get to play with the lambs?"

Haruto laughed. "If we go to his farm, I'm sure he'd let you play with the lambs."

She nodded, apparently mollified.

"Sorry," Nick mouthed silently over Melody's head. Haruto just shrugged.

"How come we can't come to the party?" Melody asked.

"Well," Nick said. "For one thing, it goes on very late. You'll be in bed before it starts, Elladee."

Melody processed that. "I could stay up late. Just this once." She tried her big brown eyes on him. Nick smiled. It had taken some time, but he'd worked up resistance on the occasions he babysat.

"Well, all we do is sit around and talk. And normally we decorate the tree, but your moms thought maybe you could help us do that before the party. And then it would be like you went to the party."

Melody's frown made it perfectly clear what she thought of that assessment, but she went back to the ornament box and pulled out one of the hunky gay mermen. She frowned.

"This mermaid is a boy."

"Yep," Nick said.

"And he has a gross moustache."

"His name is Tom," Haruto said helpfully from the couch. "He's from Finland."

"He's wearing a jacket without a shirt," Melody said. "Isn't he cold?"

"He has friends to keep him warm," Haruto said.

Nick shook his head.

"Is this one his friend?" Melody asked, picking up another one of the mermen. This one was a lifeguard. Also shirtless. It hadn't really struck Nick before how homoerotic many of the earlier ornaments had been. At least the year the giant smiling penis in the Santa hat was in the mix, he hadn't won it. He wondered if Johnny put it on their tree.

"They're all friends," Nick said. "Where should they go on the tree?" He spared a glance to Haruto, who winked at him.

Melody gave the tree another intense look, and finally agreed that the two mermen should hang near each other, down to the one side, where they'd get more sun and be warmer during the day. Nick had to admit, her kid logic was sound, though he himself wondered how any respectable merman would need a lifeguard. Didn't they breathe water?

They moved on painfully slow through the ornaments and were almost done when his landline rang. Nick left Melody to choose the next ornament and picked it up.

"We're here," Fiona said.

Nick pressed the button to buzz them in, and Fiona and Jenn came to the door a few moments later, smiling.

"How've they been?" Jenn asked.

"Reed is barely conscious," Nick said. "Haruto has been telling him stories. Elladee and I are almost done decorating the tree."

"You're still decorating the tree?" Fiona raised her eyebrows.

"She's very precise and is very adamant in me following her plan."

"There's only so much nurture can do to overrule nature," Jenn said. Fiona stuck her tongue out at her, flashing the little silver stud.

They shed coats and boots and followed him into the living room.

"I have three left," Melody said firmly. "I'm not done yet."

"There's no rush," Fiona said.

"You guys want a coffee?" Nick asked.

"You need to help me," Melody said.

"Because if you do, you know where it is." Nick grinned.

"Don't be rude, honey," Jenn said, but she said it gently.

"I'm trying to teach Nick to finish what he started," Melody said, with all the seriousness she could muster.

"I love her so very much," Haruto said. "CEO-to-be, that one."

Nick hid his chuckle with a cough. Jenn rolled her eyes.

"I'll make the coffee," Fiona said.

"Refresh, please," Haruto called after her. Fiona raised a hand to show she'd heard him.

"Remind me, before you go, that I've got...uh," Nick paused. He missed the days of being able to just spell words over Melody's head. "Colourfully packaged items for your progeny's natal soirée."

Jenn nodded. "Got it." She sat down beside Haruto and pulled Reed into her lap. He snuggled in, closing his eyes. "Oh, you're beat; aren't you, kid?"

"He's been an angel," Haruto said.

"Just like Lucifer," Nick said.

"Last one, Uncle Nick," Melody said. "This needs to go on the top branch."

He took the slightly crumpled blue paper crane from her and showed it to Haruto before he put it at the top of the tree. Haruto smiled. Nick stepped back from the tree and nodded at Melody.

"Best tree yet," he said.

"If there's a mermaid in the game, will you get it for me?" Melody asked. Then she frowned. "But only if it's a girl. I don't like boys."

"I'm a boy," Nick said.

"You're a *man*," Melody said, with infinite patience.

"Mermaids are the new princesses," Jenn said. "And dolphins are the new ponies. It's been a major paradigm shift at our house, let me tell you."

"Well, I guess Ariel does pull double duty as a princess and a mermaid, right?" Haruto said.

"Ariel makes poor choices," Melody said. "She gives up her voice for a boy."

"That's my girl," Fiona said, carrying in three cups of coffee. She handed one to Jenn and one to Haruto and then sat on the chair.

"But I like Flounder," Melody said.

Nick smiled. "Me, too. And if there's a mermaid, I'll make sure it ends up on your tree." He made a mental note to check the Christmas shop after his next shift. He looked at the tree again, pulled out his cell to take a picture, and saw he had an e-mail. He tapped his screen and then froze, biting his lip.

It was from his publisher. The subject was "Pitch."

He opened the e-mail.

"They want my novel," he said.

It took the others a few seconds to realize what he'd said. He turned, grinning. Jenn was smiling, Fiona threw a fist in the air, and Haruto was clapping. Reed stirred and frowned, and Melody looked up at him.

"What's a novel?"

"It's a book. A whole book." He knelt down to be eye to eye with her.

"Like your other book?" she asked.

"No," he said. "That book had a bunch of stories in it. This is one big story."

"Can I read it?"

"Well, I haven't finished it yet. I sent in a pitch,

and…" He trailed off, and looked at the e-mail again. "Oh. Oh, wow."

"What's wrong?" Haruto asked.

"They want the manuscript by the beginning of September." Anxiety knotted in his stomach. Short stories were one thing, but a novel? In eight months? What had he been thinking? "That's…soon."

"You're going to be fine," Fiona said. "You can do it." She rose. "This is awesome, Nick. Be excited. Worry about the hows tomorrow. Today, celebrate."

He nodded. She was right. He looked at Haruto.

"This is your fault, anyway."

"I accept all blame," he said. "If it gets me a novel. First dibs on reading the rough draft."

"Nope," Nick said. "And no going behind my back for art or anything like that."

Haruto just smiled. "We'll see."

"It's not my first book," Nick said. "I don't know why I'm so worked up."

"I mean this with a lot of respect," Haruto said. "But short stories don't get a whole lot of love. Your short story collection was lovely, and I adored it. A lot of people did. But it doesn't get the same attention as a novel will. That's different. It's your first *novel*." He raised his coffee cup. "Here's to wishes coming true."

They raised their cups. Nick, though, was remembering a wish he'd made years ago.

It hadn't had anything to do with a novel.

FOURTEENTH CHRISTMAS

"Check out the pure adventure that is my life: I leave one place with a man glued to a computer and go to another place with a man glued to his computer," Haruto said. "How's it going?"

Nick barely glanced up from the screen. "If I power through right until I go to bed, I'll get it finished. Line edits *suck*." He rubbed his eyes. He'd been at his desk for most of the afternoon. This was his last chance—he knew better than to try to work on it before or after work, not this close to Christmas.

"I brought you takeout," Haruto said. "I even got you chicken balls, with that awful red sauce. There's enough here for you to have dinner tonight and lunch tomorrow, since I bet you haven't even thought about what you're going to take tomorrow for work."

Nick finally turned away from the computer, lowering the screen. He knew Haruto would peek if he had the opportunity, and he was holding fast to not letting him see it until it was finished. He was too nervous about the book to let him see it before it was as good as he could make it. He looked at Haruto now, and sure enough, he stood in his kitchen with a brown paper bag. Nick's stomach rumbled.

"I hadn't. Thank you for doing this. If I stopped, I'm not sure I'd be able to start again, and this is pretty much my last chance."

"Well, I still want to read it, and you won't let me read it until it's printed, so…" Haruto raised the brown bag.

"You're the best," Nick said.

Haruto smiled. "I know. I bet you haven't had anything to eat since breakfast."

"Guilty."

"Well, don't forget to eat something once you're done." He put the bag on the counter. "Silas is the same."

"But somehow he's still the perfect roommate."

"He cooks me breakfast every day, and we get to live in an apartment over Bittersweets. What's not perfect about that?"

"Fair enough," Nick said.

"Also, he wants me to ask when we get to play D&D again."

"Oh. *He* wants to know, does he?" Nick couldn't help but smile. Their gaming group was a fairly new thing, but he enjoyed being their DM. It was a lot like writing, only without any sort of control over the main characters. Trying to come up with ways to confound Haruto's delightfully sneaky warlock was definitely one of the highlights.

"Fine," Haruto said. "It's me. I want to know. It's fun, okay? You were right."

"As soon as these edits are done and Christmas is done, we'll schedule it. I promise."

"Good," Haruto said. "Because I need me my quality warlock time. Do you need anything else?"

"No," Nick said. He paused. "Well, probably a shower."

"I didn't like to say," Haruto said. "But maybe squeeze that in before bed, too."

"I'll try. Hey, it's Christmas Day with Phoebe and Dennis this year, right?"

"Yes. They're hosting. Brunch at eleven." Haruto walked over to him and rested his hands on Nick's shoulders, giving them a gentle squeeze. Nick groaned, and Haruto started to massage harder. "If you were to open your e-mail, you'd know that already."

"I turned off my Wi-Fi so I wouldn't get distracted."

Haruto let out a little grunt and worked his shoulders some more. Nick gave in, closing his eyes for just a few seconds as Haruto worked out the knots that had settled in there all day.

"You need to write more and work less," Haruto said. It was a common refrain.

"I can't live off short stories. And the novel took me a year." Nick exhaled. "You are so good at this."

"I've had lots of practice. My dad's neck used to seize, and Kevin was a mess after a long day on the farm." He rubbed at a particularly stubborn knot, and it was all Nick could do not to moan.

"Well, thank you," Nick said.

Haruto stopped and then leaned over the back of his chair, wrapping his arms around Nick. He squeezed, putting his head on Nick's shoulder, and Nick wrapped his own arms around Haruto's.

"Take care of yourself. If you need anything, you call me. You're almost done. You can make it."

Nick held on to Haruto a moment longer and then let go. He nodded. There was a warmth spreading through his chest, and—if he was honest with himself—it had nothing to do with his exhaustion.

"Okay," Haruto said and stepped back. "I need to go feed Celine before she decides to shred Silas's curtains. Again. I'll see you Christmas Day, Mr. Famous Author."

"Definitely," Nick said.

Haruto let himself out, and Nick pulled the screen back up with a sigh. The line edits for the last pages of his novel crawled by. It was tedious, and hard to maintain concentration—this wasn't a reread, or the editing for narrative or grammar—this was the last hunt for any stray typos or mistakes before the book went to printing and the various e-formatting styles, and Nick constantly had to stop himself from just reading the words, rather than looking at them for any potential mistakes. He'd read the whole book out loud the first time through and found a couple of mistakes that way, and the template now had twenty-one items listed. Little things, like incorrect punctuation, or the word "so" where it should have been "do." He rubbed his eyes. The smell of the Chinese food was beyond tempting, but he soldiered on.

When he finally hit the last line of text, he rolled his head back and raised both hands in the air.

"Done!" he crowed.

He ate standing up by the sink, with the various containers opened across the countertop, digging into them with a fork as he went. It wasn't pretty, but it was faster than serving. He didn't even mind the food was only lukewarm.

This was probably the glamorous life of a novelist he'd heard so much about.

When he'd eaten way too much, he closed all the lids and shoved everything into his fridge, before he went back to the computer. He turned the Wi-Fi back on and loaded up his e-mail. Stacia, his editor, had included a checklist for him, and he brought it up on his screen one more time. He clicked the little checkbox to say he'd gone through the line edits, before adding the final file to an e-mail to send to her. Then he noticed there was one item not checked off.

Dedication.

Crap. Right. That.

He double-clicked the template file from the folder and it opened up. It was filled in with sample text.

"Dedication—To my awesome parents, wonderful partner, but more than those, the only person ever to put them to shame with sheer brilliance and astounding good looks: my editor."

Nick laughed out loud. God, he loved working with Stacia. He wondered if she sent this to all the authors she worked with. Then his smile faded. Awesome parents? Wonderful partner?

Yeah. Not so much.

He deleted the sample text, renamed the file for his novel, saved it, and then stared at the blank screen. After a long moment of realizing he had no idea what he wanted to say, he got out of his chair and walked the length of his apartment. Outside, the Ottawa night was dark, but the falling snow was catching the street lights, and the snow that had already fallen seemed to glow. He looked at his Christmas tree and hunted until he found the ornament he'd won in this year's game—a beautiful hand-spun glass orb that Phoebe had picked up from FunkArt. He smiled. Handmade gifts had heart. It was fitting the last few moments of work on the book were now. The book had been inspired by this tree and these ornaments. He'd been so unsure about whether or not his publisher—who, admittedly, had had a decent if not spectacular success with his short fiction collection—would want the book. But the idea had been in his notebook for a while and wouldn't let go. If it was a bit biographical, well, there was nothing wrong with that, and Stacia had helped him craft it into something he was pretty sure was the best thing he'd ever written.

He even liked the cover, which had driven Haruto mad not to work on.

As though drawn there by the thought of Ru's name, Nick's eyes found the blue paper crane near the top of the tree. Then the mouse with the typewriter. Mermen. A crocheted snowflake.

A thought occurred to him. It was a crazy thought, and he almost dismissed it right out of hand, but the more he looked at the paper crane, the more it settled. Warmth was spreading through his chest, and he could feel his heart thudding.

Could he do it? Could he *actually* do it? Because if it turned out badly, then it would be kind of a massive—not to mention public—failure. It would be embarrassing and humiliating and...

And it would be over. That was the really scary thing, wasn't it? That it would break something that had been important to him for, God, more years than he wanted to think about. More than a decade, at the very least. He did the mental math.

Fourteen years. Almost fifteen.

Nick took a deep breath, and then he went back to his computer. He wrote the words, saved the file, and attached it to the email.

When he clicked send, a weight seemed to lift from his shoulders.

Okay, he thought. *There goes everything.*

FIFTEENTH CHRISTMAS

Wrapped in a housecoat, Nick padded barefoot into his kitchen and set the coffeemaker on. As it started to gurgle and chug, he popped some cinnamon-and-raisin bagels into the toaster and pulled out the cream cheese. He nodded to himself and then stepped through into the living room, smiling at the decorated tree. He crouched down low, reached among the presents, and plugged it in. It lit with white lights, festive among all the ornaments and candy canes that covered the branches. He tapped one of the mermen—the shirtless cowboy—as he rose, making him swing back and forth.

Despite everything that made Christmas painful and crazy and difficult—the relentless advertising telling him how important family was, the Christmas retail season at the store and the work schedule that came with it, the commute through the ever-worsening Ottawa weather—despite it all, he wouldn't trade the day itself for anything. This quiet, as lovely as it was, was all the more special knowing that later in the morning his small house would be full of people. Maybe some things hadn't turned out anything like he'd originally hoped, but there were always these golden things—friends, stories, the tree full of memories he'd made on his own and with his chosen family. And, most important of all of those things, there was—

"Coffee," Haruto grunted, walking into the kitchen. His eyes were only slightly cracked open. "Coffee. Now." His hair—the tips dyed a seasonal bright red—was a scattered mess, and he wore rumpled Sailor Moon py-jama bottoms. They rode low on his lean hips. His bare chest was as smooth and lovely as ever. Celine wan-dered between his feet, the little black cat purring loudly, expecting breakfast.

"Good morning, handsome man," Nick said. He went back to the kitchen and poured Haruto a cup of coffee. Haruto took it from him and had a long drink. His eyes opened a bit more, and judging there was enough coffee to make it safe, Nick snuck a kiss on the back of Haruto's neck and slid his arms around him, pulling him tight.

"Good morning," Haruto said, leaning back. He drank more coffee.

The bagels popped up.

"I was going to bring you breakfast in bed," Nick said, stepping back.

Haruto jerked a thumb over his shoulder. "It's *so* not

too late. See you there." He turned and walked back out of the kitchen, and Nick laughed at his retreating back. Haruto was many things, but he was *not* a morning person.

After feeding the cat, Nick took some time making up a breakfast tray. He poured orange juice and put the bagels and cream cheese together with a bit more care than he usually would. By the time he'd assembled the tray—complete with a fresh cup of coffee for Haruto, who would likely be done with his first cup by now, assuming he hadn't fallen asleep again—he was biting his lip.

He took a deep breath and pulled out the small wrapped box from his pocket, and put it on the tray with everything else. Then, he lifted the tray and carried it through to the bedroom.

Haruto hadn't fallen back to sleep. Instead, he had his glasses on and was reading Nick's novel. Again. It hadn't moved from Haruto's bedside since he'd moved in. Since they'd gotten together. Since it had been released.

Nick grinned. "What you readin'? Any good?"

Haruto shrugged one shoulder. "It's okay. But this first page is the best part."

Nick carefully lowered the tray over Haruto, who lifted the book long enough for Nick to put it down, and then held it steady while Nick got back into bed beside him.

"Oh yeah?" Nick said.

"Yeah," Haruto said. He reopened the book to the dedication, and in a clear voice, he read, "*For Ru. I love you.*" He looked over his glasses at Nick. "Economy of words is a big deal in literature. Five words, but it really says so much."

"Wow," Nick said. "That Ru guy must be really lucky. A whole book, just for him?"

"I'll bet he wants more than one," Haruto said. "Just a hunch."

"Uh-huh."

"Hey," Haruto said.

Nick looked at him.

"Love you, too."

Nick smiled.

"What's this?" Haruto said, noticing the little package on the tray.

Nick's smile wavered. "It looks like a present. Maybe you should open it. But you need to be careful with the wrapping paper. It's part of the gift."

Haruto raised an eyebrow, but he picked up the small package and—carefully—undid the wrapping. Underneath the silver foil, around the package, a small stack of paper came free, each different bright colours and pretty patterns.

"So," Nick said, trying hard not to let his voice shake and putting the little box aside. "I thought you could teach me how to make a paper crane."

Haruto grinned. "Of course I can. Here." He handed Nick one of the pieces of paper, and together, Haruto explaining every step, they made two paper cranes. It took a while on the bed, and they had to put the tray on the bedside table and grab two books to use as a hard surface, but eventually, they had two cranes. Haruto's was by far the prettier of the two, but Nick's wasn't completely without merit.

"Okay," Nick said. "Open it."

Haruto opened the box and stared. The rings were simple, both gold bands, but both had a subtle braided rope pattern etched into their surface. Mouth open, Haruto looked at Nick.

"So, by my count," Nick said, holding up his paper crane, "we're going to need nine hundred and ninety-seven more of these." He tilted his head. "Assuming we can count the one on the tree."

"Is this...?" Haruto said. "Are you...?"

"Marry me." Nick's voice was calmer than he felt. His heart was racing and his palms were sweaty enough that he thought he might ruin the folded paper in his hand. "I mean, do you want to marry me?" He blushed. "I guess I should have phrased that in the form of a question, not a demand, but—"

Haruto kissed him. The paper cranes fell onto the blanket, and Nick took Haruto's face in his hands, the kiss deepening. The promise of a whole world rested in that kiss. Nick's whole world. Finally, Haruto broke it off, pulling back.

"You're nuts if you think I'm going to fold a thousand paper cranes," Haruto said.

"Not even five hundred," Nick said. "I'll make half." He raised an eyebrow. "Also, I'm still hanging here. I mean, I asked you a question, and I sort of need an answer."

Haruto laughed.

"No, I'm serious," Nick said. "I've got the receipt for those rings, and the manager at the jewellery store is a friend, so I'm sure he'd cut me some slack on the return policy if it's a no."

"Yes," Haruto said.

"Yes?"

"Yes."

Nick picked up the box and pulled out the first ring, and reached for Haruto's hand, but Haruto held up one finger, making Nick pause.

"One thing, though. When it comes to planning the wedding?"

"Uh-huh?" Nick said, waiting.

"*I'm* in charge," Haruto said. "Not my mom, not Fiona, not Phoebe, not even you, who I love deeply, but let's be fair, surprise declarations via book dedications aside, you're pretty risk averse. *Me.*"

"Trust me," Nick said, taking Haruto's hand and sliding the ring onto his finger. "I had no illusions."

Haruto nodded. "Good." He pulled the second ring from the box and smiled. "How about you? You wanna marry me?"

"I do."

Haruto kissed him, and Nick drew out the kiss as

long as he could. When they finally came up for air, Haruto put the ring on his finger and then rolled onto his back, holding his hand up in the air, looking at the ring. He turned and smiled at Nick. "Hey," he said.

Nick raised an eyebrow.

"This?" Haruto said. "Best Christmas ever."

"Nah," Nick said. "Just the best so far."